A House for Mack Mouse

by Liza Charlesworth

ISBN: 978-1-338-89044-0

Designer: Cynthia Ng; Illustrated by John Lund

1 2 3 4 5 6 7 8 9 10   68   31 30 29 28 27 26 25 24 23 22

Printed in Jiaxing, China. First printing, January 2023.

Once upon a time,
there was a furry brown mouse.
His name was Mack.
Mack lived with a nice family
in a cozy hole in their house.

Mack loved to sit in his little chair
and read his favorite book.
He loved to sip tea and eat cheese.
Mmmmmmmmmmmmm.
Life was delightful!

Well, life was delightful...
until a pet cat joined the family.
The cat liked Mack.
But Mack did NOT like the cat.

So, while the cat took a nap,
Mack packed his suitcase and left.
"Squeak, squeak!" he cried sadly.
"It's time for this furry brown mouse
to find a new house."

5

Scurry, scurry! Hurry, hurry!
Mack dashed up and down hills
and all around town.
Would he ever find a new home?

By and by, Mack saw a golden hive.
Would a hive make a nice house
for a furry brown mouse?
There was only one way to find out:
Mack would have to give it a try.

Oh, my! The hive was busy, busy, busy!
And it was full of sticky honey.
"Squeak, squeak!" cried Mack.
"A hive is a nice house for bees,
but it is NOT right for me."

By and by, Mack saw a nest of sticks.
Would a nest make a nice house
for a furry brown mouse?
There was only one way to find out:
Mack would have to give it a try.

Oh, my! The nest did not have a roof.
When the wind blew, it was very cold.
"Squeak, squeak!" cried Mack.
"A hive is a nice house for birds,
but it is NOT right for me."

By and by, Mack saw a craggy cave.
Would a cave make a nice house
for a furry brown mouse?
There was only one way to find out:
Mack would have to give it a try.

Oh, my! The cave was dark and spooky.
When Mack turned on his flashlight,
he saw lots of upside-down eyes!
"Squeak, squeak!" cried Mack.
"A cave is a nice house for bats,
but it is NOT right for me."

Scurry, scurry! Hurry, hurry!
Mack climbed on top of a
big orange pumpkin to rest.
"Squeak, squeak!" he cried sadly.
"Will I ever find a new house?"

Suddenly, that little mouse had a BIG idea.
"Good thing I packed my tools!" said Mack.
First, he scooped out the pumpkin seeds.
Then, he carved two fine windows
and one fine door.

At last, Mack was all done with his work.
Would a pumpkin make a nice house
for a furry brown mouse?
There was only one way to find out.
Mack opened the door and scurried inside.

"Squeak, squeak!" Mack cried happily.
"This pumpkin is cozy and bright.
It is just the right house for a mouse like me."
Then, he sat down and read his book
with a cup of tea and a bit of cheese.
Life was delightful!